Karen and the Red Shoes

written by Samantha Bloomfield
illustrated by Jane McCreary

On Friday, after school, Karen's mom took her to get some new shoes. The shoe store was crowded. Lots of kids were there with their mothers. Karen grabbed her mother's hand and pulled her over to one corner of the store.

"These are the ones!" she said, pointing to a pair of shiny red shoes. "They are so pretty!"

“I don’t know,” said her mother. “Are you sure you want those? They are very red.”

“Yes,” said Karen. “I love them!”

The shoe salesman measured Karen’s foot. Karen tried on the red shoes in her size. Then she got to wear them home.

When Karen and her mom got home, there was Tracey, her older sister, waiting in the living room.

"Oh, Mom!" shouted Tracey. "How could you let Karen get those shoes? She looks like a clown!"

“Now you stop that right now, young lady!” said her mom, carrying the bags upstairs.

“I do not look like a clown,” said Karen. “These are shoes for a princess!”

“Are you supposed to be the princess?” asked Tracey.

“Yes!” said Karen.

“Well, you could be a princess of the clown people!” said Tracey. “You could rule a whole world of clowns!”

“Very funny!” said Karen. She ran upstairs to her room. She sat on her bed and looked at her shoes. They were pretty. Tracey was wrong!

That night when Dad came home, they all went out to a restaurant called The Golden Palace. Karen wore her new shoes.

At dinner, the family talked about Thanksgiving, which was coming up next week. Their aunt and uncle and cousins would be staying in town for the week. They were all trying to come up with things the whole family could do together.

Tracey said, “Maybe Princess Clown can do some clown tricks for everybody!”

“Ha ha!” said Karen. “You’re just jealous. You wish you had new shoes, too!”

“No,” said Tracey. “No way. I don’t want to look like a clown!”

“I don’t look like a clown! Stop saying that!”

“Yes, you do. Your shoes are the perfect clown shoes!”

“Girls, that’s enough!” said their dad. Tracey and Karen just glared at each other.

Over the weekend, the girls did nothing but fight.

Karen tried to read a book in their room, but Tracey kept bothering her.

“Are you studying more clown tricks, clown girl?”

“I don’t care what you say. You’re just jealous!” She looked down at her shoes and smiled.

“Why would I be jealous of you, clown girl?”

“I’m leaving!” said Karen.

“Fine!” said Tracey.

Karen took her book and read in the living room instead. It was a book about a princess.

On Monday morning, the girls got ready for school. Karen put on her favorite dress and her new red shoes.

When she came downstairs, Tracey said, “Here she comes—Princess Clown!”

Their mother said, “Now, I mean it. Not another word about those shoes! Okay?”

“Okay,” said Tracey and Karen together slowly.

Their mom handed the girls their lunches and kissed them good-bye.

Tracey and Karen left for school together. Tracey talked to her friend Melissa the whole way. Karen walked behind them.

Soon they arrived at the schoolyard.

Julie, a girl from Tracey's class, marched right up to them.

"Hey," she said, pointing at Karen's red shoes. "Look at the clown!"

Some kids turned around and stared at Karen's shoes.

Karen could feel herself starting to cry. Tracey looked at Karen. She could see how Karen felt.

Tracey looked Julie right in the eyes. Then she said, “Well, I think her shoes are really pretty!”

Karen looked up at her sister, surprised.

Melissa said, “Yeah, they are kind of nice.”

Then all the girls wanted to see Karen’s new red shoes.

Just then the bell rang. Everyone started to go inside. Karen just stood there. So did Tracey.

"I mean," began Tracey. "Clowns wear really big shoes. Yours are just right. I think a princess could wear shoes like that."

Karen smiled up at her sister. They walked into school together and did not say another word.